TRAIL OF VENGEANCE

WORKS BY TY'RON W. C. ROBINSON II

<u>BOOKS/SHORT STORIES</u>

DARK TITAN UNIVERSE SAGA

MAIN SERIES

Dark Titan Knights
The Resistance Protocol
Tales of the Scattered
Tales of the Numinous
Day of Octagon
Crossbreed
Heaven's Called
The Oranos Imperative
Underworld

<u>*Forthcoming*</u>

Magicks and Mysticism
The Resistance vs. The Enforcement Order

COLLECTIONS

Dark Titan Omnibus: Volume 1
Dark Titan Omnibus: Volume 2
Dark Titan One-Shot Collection

SPIN-OFFS

In A Glass of Dawn: The Casebook of Travis Vail
Maveth: Bloodsport
The Curse of The Mutant-Thing
Trail of Vengeance

<u>*Forthcoming*</u>

War of The Thunder Gods
Maveth vs. The Swordman

ONE-SHOTS

Maveth, The Death-Bringer
Mystery of The Mutant-Thing
Shade & Switchblade
Retribution of Cain
The Mythologists
Ambush Bot
Kang-Zhu
Cheeseburger Man
Tessa Balthazar

THE HAUNTED CITY SAGA

The Legendary Warslinger: The Haunted City I
Battle of Astolat: A Haunted City Prequel (KOBO Exclusive)
Redemption of the Lost: The Haunted City II
Consequences of the Suffering: The Haunted City III (Forthcoming)
Helper's Hand: A Haunted City One-Shot

SYMBOLUM VENATORES

Symbolum Venatores: The Gabriel Kane Collection
Hod: A Symbolum Venatores Book
Symbolum Venatores: War of The Two Kingdoms
Symbolum Venatores: Elrad's Chronicles
Symbolum Venatores: Mystery of the Magician (Forthcoming)
Symbolum Venatores: Twilight of the Gods (Forthcoming)

A **DARK TITANS** UNIVERSE SAGA SPINOFF

TRAIL OF VENGEANCE

TY'RON W. C. ROBINSON II

CONTENTS

THE LONE OUTLAW: TARGETED

1875. An old town in the Northern West of Canada. Four men dressed in dirty suits and hats exit out of a nearby saloon. They laugh and yell at each other. Enjoying the company. Each of the hats were a different color to differentiate the four men from those outsides of their circle. From the looks of them, they maintained control over the entire town. From the sheriff's department to the poorest one in the town. Their hats were gray, brown, white, and black.

"We've done everything we could've possibly achieved." The Black Hat said.

"In this town we have." The White Hat responded. "Yet, we haven't found him yet."

"I'm sure he'll come across our path sooner than later." The Brown Hat said. "He has to. You know the mindset of a man like him. Full of anger and yet, no direction."

"You really believe what you've spewed from your mouth?"

"What else can you describe such a man like him?"

"Men like him make no mistakes. Their mind is always set on the mission. Until the mission is fulfilled, they're never satisfied.

Never."

"He'll show himself." The Gray Hat said with vigor. "Trust my words, boys."

From their left, they could hear footsteps. Boots touching the ground with a clicking sound following the steps. Coming across them in the distance is a brown horse with its rider. The horse ran toward the four hats and stopped within only a few feet from their faces. The four hats were concerned and unaware as to who's riding the horse. Truthfully, the only thing that peaked their interests was the horse and the potential to have the rider join their circle.

The rider removed himself from the horse, dressed in all brown clothing with a black duster and hat. His face was hidden by the brim of the hat and his hands were set on his sides. He started to walk toward the four hats and they still weren't sure of what to make of the whole scene. The man in the brown hat stepped up toward the rider.

"Who the hell are you supposed to be?"

"Why you hide your face from us?" The Gray Hat referenced with a grin. "Show your damn face so we can know who you are, boy."

The rider stopped and started at the four men. His face still hidden and his hands motionless on his sides. The man with the black hat stepped forward to the rider. Their faces near one another. The rider was not moved by the man's presence.

"Listen and listen good. Show us your face. You have nothing to lose. Besides your horse, of course."

"Enough of this." The White Hat yelled. "Quit playing hide and seek with us and show us your face. Who are you? Tell us your name."

"The Lone Outlaw." The Rider replied.

The four men shook in their boots. Taking minor steps back from the rider. They've heard of him across the Northern West. What he's done and the things he can do if necessary.

"It's... It's him." The Black Hat trembled in his speech. Pointing at the rider.

The rider swiftly moved his right hand, shoving his duster back and revealing his holster. From there, he fired shots at the man in the black hat, killing him with shots to the chest. He continued from there, turning toward the men in the brown and gray hats.

"Anything you wish to say?"

"You son of a-" The man in the brown hat yelled.

The rider fired once more, hitting the man in the brown hat through the chest. His eyes glared onto the man in the gray hat. Both standing completely still, their pistols directed to one another. The man in the gray hat quickened in his steps. Shuffling the pistol in his hand. The rider watched him tremble.

"You're going to turn yourself over-"

The rider shot the man in the gray hat with the pistol and he fell to the ground, lying next to the men in the brown and black hats. Their hats sat on the ground motionless to the coming wind. The man in the white hat stared down at his fallen partners of their circle. His eyes moved slowly to face the rider, who's pistol was already aimed for him.

"You're the last man standing."

"What's it to you? You killed my boys!"

"Are you concerned?"

"Listen here, you're the guy we were discussing days prior. Yet, they were right. You brought yourself over to us and killed them. Killed the believers and left the unbeliever alive. All I ask of you right now is to turn yourself in for the crimes you've committed, and these murders are added to that list of crimes."

"I haven't done anything wrong."

"Have you now? Look around, boy! Look at what you've done to these three gentlemen."

"I've done this land a service. A great service."

"You've only committed three murders. That's all you've done right now. My boys were right, you're one crazy bastard."

"Good." The rider said.

"I have no choice." The White Hat said, reaching over to his holster. "You've given me no other choice, boy, but to put you down."

The rider fired at the man in the white hat. The gunshot blasted through his head, leaving a hole through the white hat as it fell to the ground. The dirt began to hover in the air as the wind started to pick up. The rider gazed around, feeling the chilling air coming. He looked down at the man in the white hat's body and spat on him.

"Justice and vengeance are all that is left for me in this world. I can only choose one of them. And I have chosen vengeance."

The rider climbed atop his horse and rode away as thunder started to roar in the clouds above the small town. The bodies of the four men remained on the ground as the rain started to fall.

TRAIL OF VENGEANCE

LATE TRAVELS

The rain fell over the dead bodies of the Four as the Rider rode off. Sometime later, the city began to hear of more stories surrounding the famed mysterious rider. Hearing of his heroic actions across all of Canada and portions into the northern United States.

Silver City is one of the top cities of the nation. It glistened like a ghost town, but it was filled with people. Riders rode through the muddy streets on their horses as prostitutes stand on the corners. One horse in particular, white, is coming up to the City Hall building. The horse stopped and its rider leaped off. The rider was known in the city as Jack London. A young, handsome gentleman to many of the women and a potential apprentice and ally toward the men. He made his focus toward the City Hall. Jack entered, going up the stairs, passing by visitors throughout the building. Reaching the second floor, Jack had stepped into the main office.

"Governor." Jack said, standing at the desk.

In front of Jack was a desk, surrounded by soldiers and behind the desk sat a man of African descent. His position in the Hall was deemed unpopular to a few of the city's residents. His countenance was clear as was his purpose for his place. Brute, fierce, and born to lead. This man was Lieutenant Cullen Mason. Realizing the Lieutenant was sitting in the governor's desk, Jack stepped back with confusion. Cullen raised his hand, relaxing Jack.

"The governor isn't here at the moment. As you can see."

"Where is he?"

"Do not worry. I will be taking his place until he returns."

"Returns? Where did he go?"

"Some important business. Seemed like a family matter."

"I understand. Well, sorry sir. Btu, I've come here with some urgent news."

"I would expect it nonetheless. Why else would you be here. So, what have you come to tell me?"

"There was a quadruple-murder near the area of Yukon."

"Yukon?" Cullen said, leaning back. "The causalities? Their names?"

"Names were unknown. But, we do know the killer."

"And this killer is?"

"The people call him The Lone Outlaw."

"The Lone Outlaw." Cullen nodded. "An interesting title to proclaim for a mysterious figure."

"I guess you've heard of him before." Jack said.

"Indeed I have. My soldiers have heard the stories of this Outlaw going throughout the country. Saving lives and not even taking a ounce of gold for his troubles. Seems like a folktale to me. But, you've come with news of his presence nearby. He's probably come into the city without us even knowing."

"What's should we do?"

Cullen waved his hands and the soldiers took their leave out of the office. With only Jack and Cullen in the office, Cullen offered Jack a seat and Jack kicking his legs went and took the seat. Once Jack was comfortable in the chair, Cullen stood up out of his and approached Jack directly.

"Keep it simple. Keep a lookout for this lone outlaw. We must capture him."

"Capture him?" Jack wondered. "I thought we were only going to find him and see why he's helping people."

"No. the man's a criminal. An enemy of us all. His little acts of heroism could easily be turned into acts of an invader. We don't even know if he was even born in this country. Let alone if his actions as pure. Track him down as best as possible. I will do what I can on my end. Once we find him, everything will show itself."

"I'm sure you have something in mind to find him?"

"As a matter of fact I do. I've already sent out one of our most trusted men to the location where this Outlaw is claimed to reside. Once he finds him, all our answers will be certain."

"I understand you clearly, sir."

"And what of the other one? Thaine Tucker."

"What of him?"

"Has there been anything of him recently? Any sightings or encounters?"

"None that we've come to discover."

Cullen nodded and returned to his seat.

"Very well. You may go."

"Yes sir."

Jack turned and left from the office. Cullen leaned forward to the desk with his hand on his chin. Thinking.

An individual rode upon a black horse, entering the small area of Maverick Town. A gruff-looking man with eyes of a vicious killer. His dirty brown duster looked to mix with the ground. The people in the area call him Thaine Tucker. Tucker entered through the shining lights of the Maverick Town street. Thaine rode into the city, yet no one recognized him. Not even with his face clearly seen. He took this as an opportunity to make his name known amongst them. His appearance with a full-grown beard seemed to impress the women. Thaine watched them as they exited through a building. Looking at its structure and hearing the faint sound of music coming through the doors, Thaine knew it was a brothel and bar. Making his stop, he stepped off from the horse and walked into the building.

Thaine glanced through the interior of the brothel, catching nothing but bare-chested women surrounding the bar and tables. He grinned as he walked through, so did the women. One woman, proceeded to approach him, donning a silky white dress, a dress which quickly caught the eyes of Tucker as he removed his hat.

"Looks like you've come here to find a good time."

"A good time can be anytime, milady. However, right now is not so. I'm here looking for a Mr. Jonathon Wayne. Is he here?"

"Lucky for you, he's here." She moved in closer with a smile. "Follow me."

Thaine went and followed the prostitute down the hallway past the bar, seeing several doors on both sides. Watching her steps, Tucker knew the prostitute was leading him to the main office. How Tucker knew where the office was within the brothel was something he kept to himself. Not everyone can know the methods of Thaine Tucker. Standing in front of the door, hearing the music in the background. She knocked. Within a second, she heard the response to enter as did Tucker.

They entered the office and the prostitute walks over to the desk. Sitting at the desk was a handsome, arrogant man, wearing his favorite brown suit and cowboy hat. He raised his head, looking up toward the prostitute and behind her he saw Tucker.

Thaine grinned.

"Mr. Jonathan Wayne, I presume."

"That I am." Wayne said, turning to the prostitute. "Woman, who have you led into my office?"

"Sir, he requested to see you by name."

Wayne nodded as he looked unimpressed. He sighed and waved his hand.

"Thank you otherwise. Please sir, come and sit."

"That I will do."

Thaine went and sat down in front of the desk, facing Wayne. The prostitute stood by the door, watching the two men staring at one another. The tension in the air began to make her uncomfortable. Wayne's eyes leaned over to the prostitute and he saw her standing with a slight shiver. he smiled and told her to leave. She went and shut the door.

"So, tell me sir, who are you and why have you come to see me?"

"Because, you're the owner of this establishment. I'm here to collect my share of the profit."

"Your share? Share of what?"

"The hell do you think? I made an agreement with the previous owner of this place and we settled on a fifty-fifty deal. Such was a simple agreement. I see now, you're the new owner and I believe you should keep this deal. No need to cause trouble."

"Trouble? By you?"

"Who else?"

Wayne scoffed.

"For starters, the previous owner never told me of a co-partner in the business. So tell me, just who the fuck are you supposed to be?"

"Who the fuck am I? I'm Thaine Tucker."

Wayne leaned closer, staring at Tucker. He rubbed his eyes

and continued to stare. Tucker shook his head and waved around his hat.

"Looking for something?" Tucker laughed.

"Oh shit. Tucker? Oh! I remember now. I didn't recognize you with the beard."

"It's a recent growth. So, you do know of me?"

"I do. The previous owner, Mr. Barnes had informed me of another partner who shared a stake in this place. He only referred to them as Tucker. Never told me your first name."

"Because we spoke on business terms. Last names only."

"I see. I see. So, you've come here to collect your share of the place?"

"Why else would I have come?"

"Well, I could. But, as all businesses work, once a new owner is in place, the previous deals do not continue further."

"You're telling me I came all this way for nothing?"

"Yes. But, we could however make a deal. Between us this time."

Tucker leaned back and scoffed.

"The fuck we have to make a new deal for? I already had one and it branched over once Barnes sold the place to you. It's all part of the deal. Regardless of ownership."

"That's not how I do business."

"So I can tell."

"Look, I have an offer for you. Let's make ourselves a deal right now. Between you and I. Once the deal is in place, you will have your share and more."

"And that's supposed to be all?" Tucker waved his arms.

"And I could throw in one of the women out there. I'm sure one of them will suit you well."

"To lay down with one of the women out there? Ha! No. I never play with the product. Not my standard."

"Then, you're missing out, my friend."

"Missing out?" Tucker said. "What are you implying?"

"I've tasted my share of these women. It was the only way I could know if they were good for business."

Tucker nodded slowly, leaning stealthily toward the desk.

"Just out of curiosity, how many of these women have you laid with?"

"Five."

"Five? Ah. Five. Quite a number for a beginner."

"I know right!"

Thaine laughed with Wayne before he bolted up from the chair and fired shots into Wayne's chest four consecutive times. Wayne leaned back in the chair, touching the wounds as he moved slowly. Struggling to breathe. Thaine walked around the office, holding the revolver in his hand. He paused and turned toward Wayne.

"Oh, that's right."

Thaine fired another round at Wayne through his head. With Wayne's body hanging from the chair, Thaine placed the revolver back in its holster and let out a slow sigh.

"Five it was."

Thaine exited the office as the same prostitute who greeted him walked by and into the office. Seeing the body of Wayne in the chair, she let out a loud fearing scream. Thaine grinned as the bar and brothel visitors began to move in terror. Walking back to the outside, Tucker sat atop his horse and rode off, leaving Maverick Town in a sense of fear. A method he's too fond of.

Sometime later in Silver City, Jack sat in the saloon, taking in a drink. From the doors, the sound of clicking boots echoed, grabbing his attention. Jack looked over toward the bar and saw the dirty brown duster and hat. For a split moment, Jack believed him to be the Outlaw, only for that thought to wallow away as the Outlaw doesn't dress in such colors according to the witnesses. The stranger had his drink and sat at a table across from Jack. He drank and caught the eyes of Jack staring.

"You see something?"

"Nothing much."

The stranger scoffed. Standing up from the table, he made his move toward Jack's table and took a seat. Jack sat up with hesitance.

"I didn't ask you to sit here."

"I know and I don't give a shit. But, you're giving me strange looks and I don't take that lightly. Who are you?"

"Who are you?"

"I'm Thaine Tucker. Only the few may know me around this city. Seems today, you've become one of them."

"Tucker." Jack said. "The figurative on the run."

"Fugitive?! No boy, I'm not a fugitive. Just a businessman with certain standards which society refuses to believe."

"I've heard of all your works. The terrible things you've done."

"They're not terrible. They're practical."

"You're just like that Outlaw roaming around out there. Doing whatever it takes to live for yourself."

"Outlaw! You talk of him? Oh, you think I'm just like him, huh? Some kind of hero to the people? Well, I'm no hero. I'm the guy who gets shit done regardless of praise or hatred."

"From what I've heard, you're just a selfish man looking out for your own fame."

"You're damn right. And who the hell are you?"

"I'm Jack London and I report to Lieutenant Cullen Mason."

Thaine scoffed with a smile, clapping his hands lightly to avoid eyes from the others.

"You work for him? This is something. So, let me guess? He's sent you, his little errand boy on a mission to find me and the Outlaw, huh?"

"That's right."

"And what are your orders once you find them?"

"To bring them in. By any means."

"Oh. Any means. That's nice."

Tucker cocked his head as his hand slowly reached down toward the holster.

"You really believe you can bring me in? You can't be that dumb."

"I follow orders. It's what is required of me."

"Boy, let me give you some advice. Following orders blindly will put you into an early grave. A suggestion I might add. Don't go blind into the fight. Like you're doing right now."

Thaine's hand raised above the table. No sign of the revolver as he chuckled. Standing up from his seat as he took one last gulp. Taking his leave, Jack rose up and grabbed Tucker by his shoulder.

"I won't let you leave this bar."

"Boy, best you get your hand off my shoulder. Before you end up without it."

Jack with a slight hesitant to remove his hand, when and done so. Thaine grinned with a muffled chuckle to follow as he exited the saloon. Jack stood in the middle of the bar, seeing the eyes of the others on him. Shaking his head, he too left the saloon.

Elsewhere in the outskirts of Silver City and not far out from Maverick Town, Lieutenant Cullen's hired man, Constantine Welles rode out alone into the dark of the night, toward a deserted landscape. Scouting the area, Constantine only found an old shack with a horse standing by. Jumping from his own horse, he approached the shack through the shrouding mists and the vocals of owls, just as he made one step closer to the shack, the door bolted open like a gust of wind. Constantine quickly raised up his revolver. His eyes locked onto the entrance. Seeing nothing but a dim candlelight.

"Whoever's in there, step outside."

While he waited, the sound of creaking wood crawled up Constantine's spine as from the doorway appeared a shadow. Inching closer t the outside as the moonlight shined upon him, the figure revealed himself to be the Outlaw himself. Seeing his presence, Constantine grinned.

"Looks like you've been found."

"On what circumstances have I been discovered?"

"You know why? I've been sent here on orders to bring you in. dead or alive."

"Orders under who's authority do you follow? Mason's?"

"You know him too well and his methods."

"Best you turn around and leave." The Outlaw commanded. "No need for another death this night."

"I'm not leaving until I've completed my order."

"Son, you do not want to take this any further."

"I'm here. Therefore, I must complete what I've come for."

The Outlaw paused, gazing back toward Welles. His eyes were locked on. Welles held his position with the revolver drawn. Seeing as how Constantine did not make a move to turn away, the Outlaw sighed and kindly took his return into the shack. Taking one step inside, a round fired from Welles' revolver into the air.

"I meant what I said." Constantine spoke. "I'm taking you in. Dead or alive."

The Outlaw turned around to face Welles and the two stood at arms. Both their eyes were locked onto the other. Welles smirked, seeing the opportunity of taking out the famed Outlaw.

It appeared that's what he wanted regardless of Lieutenant Cullen's orders. The Outlaw on the other hand, only saw an intruder to his solitude. An invader who was forewarned and disregarded the decency which was allotted to him. Outlaw's hand was steady on the handle of his revolver. His demeanor ### calm. Welles began to sweat, taking the moment to wipe his forehead, both fired their shot. The air cooled while the gunfire's echoed had filtered away.

"Check your chest." The Outlaw said.

Welles looked down and felt his chest, feeling the warmth of his own blood as he glanced at his hand covered in it. His legs buckling as he stumbled to the ground. The Outlaw approached him as he raised his revolver to gain a shot. The Outlaw placed his hand over Welles' revolver and lowered it.

"I will get my shot." Welles muffled.

"No. No you will not."

Welles laid on the ground, coughing up blood as the Outlaw stood over him. Not in triumph, but in shame. In the shame of Welles' own self-will. The air was cool enough to keep Welles stable for a few seconds. Although it wouldn't have mattered much in the end. The Outlaw stood by Welles' side as his breath began to decline in minutes. Welles attempted to speak, only for the Outlaw to silence him. Suggesting he keep his breath and not to waste it on idle words.

"Should've taken my advice. I did not want to end it like this. You're not on my list."

Welles laid back as he exhaled his last breath and his blood poured from his chest. The Outlaw sighed and walked back to the shack, taking a look at Welles' horse. He nodded.

HITMAN OF THE OLD WEST

In the morning light over Silver City, a horse ran into the streets, bringing the attention of Cullen and London. The horse made its stop in front of the city hall where Cullen instantly saw a body laying over the horse. Signaling his men to retrieve the body, he and Jack watched as they removed the body from the horse. The horse shook and galloped away.

"Seems Welles did not complete the task." Cullen uttered.

"What should we do?" Jack questioned. "Should I go ahead and send out word to the men?"

"No need. I already have someone who can do the job."

"If I may ask, who do you have in mind?"

"You'll see him soon enough." Cullen answered, returning to City Hall.

Elsewhere back in Maverick Town, Thaine had overtaken the brothel and bar establishment. Countless men entered and relished in the sight of women and whiskey. Thaine walked throughout the brothel, greeting the men and seeing their lustful gazes toward the women. Thaine knew he made the right decision in his own mind. Making his return to his office, the prostitute he met previously entered and handed Thaine a paper. Grabbing it,

Thaine looked calmly. Sighing as he sat the paper down.

"Where did you get this?"

"It's what came in."

"Did you see who delivered it?"

"Some man who came by the entrance. He came and left the paper on the bar. Didn't give a name nor anything else."

Thaine nodded and glanced back at the paper.

"Thank you for giving me this."

"It's my job."

"I understand. However, one must ask. You don't seem to be afraid."

"Afraid?" She said.

"Yes. You saw Wayne's body in here. Bleeding out after I shot him. You stayed."

"Well, to be honest, I have nowhere else to go."

"No family?"

"No sir."

"Well, you have no reason to fear me. I did what had to be done. Wayne was an untruthful business partner and business had to be done. He was the only target. No one else."

"You don't have to explain it to me. I get it."

Thaine nodded with a grin.

"Sure. Sure."

Grabbing the paper again, taking another glance. Thaine sighed and laid back in the chair.

"Appears I'll be paying them a visit. Subtly."

Within the office of City Hall, Cullen sat at the desk with his men standing by at the door. Jack sat down across from the desk as Cullen began to speak with a visitor. The visitor looked almost like a wrangler. Although, not a wrangler they're familiar with.

The clicking sound emitting from his boots to his slanted hat. His countenance was somewhat of a cocky nature. Yet with confidence. His gaze would gloom over those not in his favor. Cullen began to tell him of the Lone Outlaw and the crimes he's committed. The wrangler smacked his gums and leaned in toward the desk.

"Any idea where this man is?"

"Last seen on the outskirts of town. Probably still out there. Can't have traveled far."

The wrangler gave Cullen a nod and stood up from his seat. Jack rose up from his own seat in response. From there, Cullen stood up and extended his hand.

"Do we have a deal, Mr. Duke Rogers?"

"Yeah. We have a deal."

The wrangler and Cullen shook hands with each other giving a slight nod of respect.

"How soon do you want this man turned in?" The wrangler asked.

"How soon can you move?"

"I got you. They don't call me Longshot for nothing."

With the wrangler taking his leave, Jack approached Cullen with questions concerning the man's whereabouts and his purpose for being summoned into the City Hall. Cullen quietly sat back down at the desk and sighed.

"Because Jack, that man is the key to bringing in this Outlaw. By any means."

"You're saying you gave him permission to kill the Outlaw?"

"If it comes to that, yes."

"And what if he doesn't?"

"Then he'll bring him in. look, everything is going well. The man's a mercenary-for-hire. His only motivation is to be paid in full. He's already received half. Once he finds this Outlaw and

either kills him or brings him in, he'll receive the other portion.
No need to worry. Things will work out for the better."

LADY IN RED

Moving through a mining facility in droves were a group of men. Two of them were rushing back and forth between the mine and their carriage with chests covered in locks. Tossing them in the carriage and back to the mines. While making their quick moves, one f the men held a chest and went to turn toward the carriage only to find himself in the gaze of the Outlaw. Dropping the chest to the ground, signaling the attention of the other men. They looked with stares as the Outlaw's gaze was set on the man in front of him.

"Are these chests yours?"

"Not exactly. They're for a few friends of ours. Nothing more."

"Then, why rush? Seems if they belonged to your friends as you say, you wouldn't have no need to rush."

"He's not the one in charge here." said one of the other men, stepping forward. "You see, sir, these chests, they do belong to a friend of ours. This is not a thieves' game. Only a pickup."

"A pickup? Then, why move in such speed?"

"Because our friend requested we do. So, we wouldn't run into other thieves or strangers such as yourself."

The Outlaw nodded, taking a look at his surroundings. Seeing only some trees in the distance to the mine's entrance and the sound of a train moving in the distance behind him.

"The friend you continue to speak of. What is his name?"

"I'm afraid we cannot divulge such information. Especially with those outside of the range of information."

"You have no choice. His name."

"We cannot say."

The Outlaw quickly bolted out his revolver to the forehead of the thief, startling the others as they stepped back. The thief breathed heavily feeling the coldness from the revolver against his forehead. The Outlaw's eyes remained focused. Unmoved.

"You have another opportunity to answer me. I am a just man. I kill only those necessary."

"Ok! I'll give you the name."

"I'm waiting."

"Weldon. Ray Weldon."

The Outlaw held the revolver steady and pulled it away from the thief's forehead.

"Where will I find this Ray Weldon?"

"He moves between Silver City and Maverick Town. He doesn't stay in one place."

"So, I'll have to make my rounds. That's fair enough."

The thieves remained still. Their nervous nature could be felt across the air. The Outlaw gave them a nod and placed his revolver into his holster. Cocking his head toward their carriage, he gave them leave. Without a second to pass, the thieves leaped onto the carriage and rode off. The Outlaw watched as they fled and looked down at several gold coins which were left behind after the chest's fall. picking up one of the coins and examining it, the Outlaw knew this Ray Weldon operated with some powerful people.

In Silver City, Jack went and gathered several of Cullen's armed men. Their objective was set in motion after a brief discussion with Cullen the day prior. Jack and the men prepared a search through Silver City for Thaine Tucker. With the wrangler on the hunt for the Outlaw, Cullen believed Jack would be best suited to track down Tucker and bring him in. Jack's plan was a simple one: To search every populated location in Silver City for Tucker and if they ended up finding him, they would arrest him without haste and bring him in before Cullen.

"Sir, what happens if he doesn't surrender?" One of the armed men questioned.

"Ugh." Jack breathed. "We can't just kill the man. He must be served justice."

In another distant location, the thieves who fled from the Outlaw's sight had returned to their base. Bursting inside like animals, they were quick to pause in front of their leader, Ray Weldon. A man of a brutish stature, yet his drinking would make many look in another direction. Weldon stood up, trembling the ground as he approached the thieves. Searching their hands and seeing three chests and some gold coins.

"Where's the other one?"

"The other what?"

"The damn chest! There were four."

"I dropped it."

"You dropped it?! The hell would you drop a chest full of my money?!"

"Sir, we were found."

"Found by whom? Officials? Gunslingers? What? Who?"

"Some stranger. He dressed like an outlaw."

Weldon scoffed, shaking his head as he gulped another drink.

"You mean to tell me some stranger came to you guys and you left in fear?"

"Sir, his gaze was not of this world. He had to have been some sort of ghost."

"Ghost? You saw the damn thing! He wasn't some ghost." Weldon sighed. "What is the last thing you know of him and my chest?"

"The chest is still near the mine and the stranger said he's coming to see you."

Weldon rose up and snatched the thief, tossing him outside of the base. Taking a second to catch his breath, Weldon turned around toward the others.

"It appears we have someone n our trail. Thanks to all of you. Now, I must put out the word. I have someone who will deal with this stranger while the rest of you return to the mine and collect whatever's left. Now go!"

Later in the night, the wrangler had arrived at the shack where the Outlaw and Constantine Welles had their confrontation. Moving with much quietness, the wrangler searched the shack, kicking down the door. He entered with his six-shooter aimed steady. Within the shack was only a worn-out bed, a dining table with two chairs and a closet. The air was covered with the stench of gunpowder. That was enough to confirm the workings of the Outlaw in the shack. Yet, there was no living sign of the Outlaw to return to the shack. His place there was done and he had moved on. The wrangler sighed and stepped out of the shack.

The next morning, Weldon sat inside the base with his men surrounding him. Some had prostitutes sitting on their laps. From the opening door entered a woman gowned in red. Hair as dark as the night, yet cut to the ends of her ears. Her eyes sparkled before the men and Weldon stood up to greet her.

"Our lady in red. Good of you to come."

"Nice sending out the word for my assistance. What is it you need?"

"We have a problem."

"I'm listening."

LOOT OF THE TRADE

During the mid-morning, Thaine rode into Silver City, covering himself in a cloak and gaiter. Leaving his horse across from City Hall, Thaine quickly moved across the road toward the Hall. Taking a slight moment to listen, he could hear the ongoing conversation between Cullen and Jack. Thaine smacked his gums hearing the muffled talk.

"He's still inside."

Thaine took the time to overhear the conversation. Within a mere moment of minutes, the voices stopped, following the sound of an opening door. Thaine raised his head, peeking through the window as he saw Cullen and Jack exit the office. With them no longer inside, Thaine pulled a blade from his boot and picked against the window, creaking it open. Thaine slowly entered the office and searched through the drawers of the desk. Pulling out papers detailing the ongoing events surrounding Silver City and Maverick Town.

"What is this?" Thaine questioned, reading the other paper.

Upon the paper were small, documented details of a coming war between the Northerners and the Natives of the outskirts. Thaine was unaware of the Natives, having yet to encounter them. Now knowing they're somewhere near the areas of both towns, Thaine began to question his work and methods. Seeing another opportunity on the horizon to cause more trouble for Cullen and his gang of soldiers.

"Best I take this one. Leave the rest."

Thaine quickly folded the paper into his coat and jumped from the window to the outside as a soldiers approached the door, taking a look inside. Seeing nothing, the soldier turned back and walked away. Outside, Thaine chuckled as he cocked his head and walked down the road toward the residents of Silver City.

Ray Weldon sat in leisure within his base as his men walked back and forth carrying chests filled with gold. With each man passing, Weldon grinned at the glinting speck of the coins. As he admired the continuing appearance of gold, the door to his base opened. Not expecting any visitors, Weldon sat up in his seat, seeing the silhouette of a duster and hat standing. The figure entered as the door shut behind him. From there, Weldon stood up as his men were paused in their steps. Weldon took a moment to measure the man and nodded.

"And who are you supposed to be?"

"Ask your men. They know of me."

Looking at his men, seeing sweat forming upon their foreheads as the chest in their hands started to tremble. Thinking back, Weldon knew it. He faced the man as he commanded his men to return to their duty.

"You're the bastard who threatened my men at the mine?"

"I didn't threaten them. I warned them."

"Where I'm from, talk like that is a threat. You were going to kill them and take my gold."

"I have no need of your gold. I only seek justice."

"Justice for whom?"

"For all who desire it."

Weldon laughed, facing his men with a large smile as his men chuckled softly. Hidden under their muffled mouths. Weldon pointed at the man, shaking his head after hearing his words.

"And who are you supposed to be? The savior to the Northern West?"

"I am the Outlaw who brings forth justice. Even from the crooked actions you yourself serve."

"Who do you work for? The government?"

"I work for the people. Nothing less."

"Look here, fellow. I've already been told of your actions and I have someone looking for you. A shame they're not here to take you out."

"I'm sure we'll meet soon. Everyone often does."

The Outlaw turned away toward the door. Before his hand could reach the handle, the sound of a crashing chest bolted through the base. The Outlaw slowly turned back as his right hand was pressed against his revolver's handle. Weldon remained still, shrugging his shoulders while yelling at his man to pick up the chest and gold. The Outlaw's hand pulled away from the revolver's handle and to the door. Once he opened the door, taking one step out, he paused.

"Forget something?" Weldon chuckled.

"No. only to warn you."

"Warn me of what?"

"If I catch your actions out here again, I will come for you."

The Outlaw stepped out of Weldon's base as the door closed behind him to nothing but silence. Even Weldon's men were afraid of what the Outlaw might do if he returns. However, Weldon was not afraid as he yelled again to his men to return to work. Shaking his head in annoyance of the visit, Weldon sat back down in his chair.

"Nothing to worry about." Weldon uttered. "Our assassin will take care of him. I know she will."

THE VIGILANTRESS STRIKES

Lieutenant Cullen returned to his office later in the day and quickly noticed something within was off. Glancing over at the window behind his desk, he walked over and saw the glass slightly pushed outward. His eyes widen as he never opened the window during the day nor the days prior. Yelling for Jack, the young man ran into the office to see Cullen pointing at the window.

"Someone was here." Cullen yelled. "Someone was inside my office!"

"Sir, there was no one here after we left."

"The window is pushed outward. As if someone came in from the outside."

"Are you sure, sir?"

"I am. I need to check my desk. If something is missing, it proves my point."

Opening the drawers in haste, Cullen scrambled through the papers, tossing them atop the desk and around. Jack stood still as the papers flew through the air by Cullen's speed. Reaching toward the bottom drawer, Cullen searched and quickly stopped. Taking another look inside and only responding by slamming his fist on the desk, startling Jack for a second.

"It's gone!"

"What is gone?" Jack questioned. "Sir, what is missing?"

"The damn papers! Shit! I've been robbed. Jack, send out word to the troops. Tell them to search for a thief in the city. They're still lingering around here. Be it man or woman. They must be found and brought in before me."

"Yes sir."

Cullen stormed out the office with Jack following him to the outside. As they both stepped outside, taking a gaze at the city's civilians, Jack approached three soldiers whom were standing by, telling them the details of their new mission. The soldiers took Jack's words and followed him to their horses. Watching the soldiers take their leave with Jack, Cullen took another gaze at the civilians. Watching their hand gestures and the body language. Cullen was keen to discover whom the thief could be even though he already had several conclusions in his mind.

Elsewhere in another area, the Outlaw rode through the opened desert of the north, making his way toward a location where Weldon's operations were continued. Making haste to reach the spot before the day's end, the Outlaw's horse is startled by something moving in the distance. The Outlaw paused as the horse refused to continue further.

"What is it, boy?"

The horse shook itself as it refused to continue moving forward. The Outlaw stepped from his horse with his revolver in hand, taking slow walks to see the object standing in the desert. The object stood upright just as he did. Walking closer, the Outlaw could tell it was another human being, cloaked in a black duster and brim hat.

"State your name before I have to shoot." The Outlaw stated.

"I have no name. only a purpose." said the figure.

"Your voice? You sound like a woman. You are a woman,

aren't you?"

"I am." She replied, lowering the gaiter from her face. "What business is it of yours?"

"You tell me? Why would a woman standing alone out in the desert in the path of riders? Looking for someone in particular?"

"I have my reasons."

"As do I. Best you move out of my way. No need to escalate this any further."

"I will not move. I do not know you or your business in this region. As far as I can see it, you're trespassing."

The Outlaw sighed with bitter in his breath. Looking down, he raised up the revolver and saw the woman held one of her own. He nodded with a slight smirk on his face. Her face showed a smile of her own, letting him know she was aware of his actions.

"Are you sure this is what you want to do?" The Outlaw asked.

"If I have to, yes."

"It appears we have ourselves a crossroads."

"One you brought to yourself."

"Enough of this, woman. Move aside."

"And why should I move out of your path? Who are you that I should obey your words?"

"I am the Lone Outlaw and I am on a mission to stop a criminal from continuing his work."

"The Lone Outlaw?" She said slowly. "No. you're him?"

"You're heard of me?"

"I heard of what you did in Silver City. Taking out the Four Hats on your own. Many would have never done such a task. Even if they were capable of achieving it."

"Then they are nothing but fools. Someone had to take the task and I did. Four criminals are dead and now I hunt down those who remain."

The woman nodded, removing her hat, fully exposing her fair face and blue eyes. She removed the scarf from around her neck, completely showing her smile as she placed her revolver back into its holster. She walked over toward the Outlaw and extended her hand. Looking at it, the Outlaw stayed silent as he shook her hand.

"I'm on a mission as well."

"You? On what mission requires a woman such as yourself to stand in the middle of a travel path?"

"There's someone who took something from me many years ago. I learn how to defend myself with every weapon that was within my sight. After about three years, I am here, doing my part to protect the innocent."

"And who are you hunting down?"

"Lieutenant Cullen Mason."

The Outlaw remained paused, placing his revolver back in the holster. Taking a look at their surrounding sand only seeing dirt with small fragments of grass as the wind bellowed around them. In his own mind, the Outlaw began to answer his own questions as to why the young woman would be looking to take down Lieutenant Cullen. What did he do to her that made her into the woman he's standing by. Before asking the question, she answered it without even his notice of interest. From her mouth, she stated Cullen had began a manhunt against her after their brief encounter in Silver City. Cullen set a bounty on her head and she fled into the wilderness to defend herself. Eliminating all the hunters who came for her by Cullen's command. Now, she waits for Cullen himself to arrive as she can release the final blow.

"And have many other hunters made themselves known since?"

"Not as many as before. I assume he believes I've ran too far into the United States. Otherwise, I'll be shooting down bounty hunters to this day."

"I see. I'll tell you this. The reason I'm in this area is to find a mining site that's being operated by a man called Ray Weldon. A thief stealing gold and claiming it as his own."

"There's a small town down the path. I've seen only a few men every other day taking carriages back and forth with crates of gold. Never questioned where they came and went with such a trove."

"Then this is the spot. I must confront his men and warn them of the price they might pay for Weldon's foolishness."

The woman nodded as she looked down the path toward the mine's direction. Shaking her head to her own mind, she moved aside as the Outlaw's horse walked over toward him. Petting it with a chuckle in her voice. The Outlaw went onto his horse and thanked the woman for her honesty.

"Nice horse you got there." She smiled.

"He's a keeper. One of the things I'm grateful for."

"So, what will you do once you stop the men at the mines?"

"I will speak with Weldon and give him an update concerning his work. Afterwards, I will deal with Cullen's men."

"His men? He's hunting you down too?"

"For killing the Hats. It appears we make enemies wherever we go."

"We could work together against him and his soldiers. Put it all to a stop much quicker than either of us could anticipate."

"We could." The Outlaw answered. "Yet, now is not the time."

The Outlaw moved past the young woman as she stood watching him move on the trail. The horse paused and stepped as the Outlaw turned around to face her.

"One other thing." The Outlaw said. "You never told me your name."

"My name has been lost to the desert. The people only call me the Vigilantress."

"Vigilantress? What have you done to gain such a title?"

"I have my works ahead of me."

"Appears you do." The Outlaw answered. "Do me a favor."

"Sure."

"Keep watch on this trail for any of Weldon's men. Or even Cullen's soldiers."

"I'm always on watch." She answered.

The Outlaw gave her a nod as he rode off down the path. The Vigilantress turned and walked over to the side, sitting down as she twirled the revolver around her finger.

CIVIL DUTIES AND DEATH TO RIGHTS

Riding down the path, the Outlaw had reached the small town which the Vigilantress spoke of. Passing by a small wooden sign which read, "Welcome to Maverick Town" Entering the old town, seeing people walking on with fear encompassed upon their faces, the Outlaw knew there was something oppressing the Maverick residents. While riding into the town, he looked ahead and saw three gunslingers antagonizing a lone man who was riding his cart through the street.

"I cannot allow that to continue." The Outlaw said under his breath.

Riding over towards the three men, they heard the galloping of the horse coming up behind them as they turned, seeing the Outlaw with his two six-shooters aimed and he fired upon them, killing them in front of the old man. The Outlaw's horse stopped as he leaped off and approached the old man, checking on him to see any injuries. Searching him, he found no injuries and the man was thankful for the Outlaw's sudden arrival.

"Go about your business." The Outlaw said.

With the old man thanking him before taking his leave, the Vigilantress herself rode into town, quickly coming up upon the Outlaw. Her face was in distress as she leaped from her horse and ran toward him. Tugging on his sleeve as she looked back at the entrance to the town. The Outlaw started to wonder; what was she afraid of?

"They're here!" She said. "Lieutenant Cullen's men. They're here."

"I see them." The Outlaw responded, gazing ahead at the horses entering the town with the soldiers and in front of them was Jack.

The Outlaw stepped upon his horse and faced them, leaving the Vigilantress with confusion and terror as she continued to ask him what he would do since they've arrived much earlier than she expected. The Outlaw looked down toward her and back toward Jack and the soldiers. With a nod, he informed her he would speak with them and whatever happens after will simply happen. Otherwise, the Outlaw already had business to take care of in the town regarding Weldon and his mining crew of thieves.

"What if they start shooting?" She asked.

"Then shoot back."

Riding off to meet with Jack and the soldiers, the Vigilantress stayed back near the saloon of the town and watched as the residents all gazed their eyes toward the Outlaw's rushing move to meet with them. Coming up near them as Jack ceased and the soldiers paused behind him. Jack turned back and gave the soldiers directions to follow as the Outlaw reached them in the road.

"Look who've we found." Jack grinned. "The famed Outlaw of the Northern West."

"I am not here for troubling causes. I came for a mission."

"A mission? And does that mission include killing more men?"

"Yes. Thieves who've been robbing the poor of their wealth and necessities."

"Then, let us help you in this matter. Give the people back

what's been stolen."

"I will not. If you were truly a good cause, you would've done so in Silver City. Yet, my actions there prove your words are flawed and laden with poison. However, the poison comes from your boss. You're a different lad."

"Truth be told, I am not like my boss. But, I must follow commands just as any soldier. It is our place."

"Your place. Not mine."

Jack shook his head and nodding before facing the Outlaw once more.

"Look, we didn't come here to start a shootout. We've come to find a woman. The people call her the Vigilantress. Might as well ask you if you've seen her through your travels?"

"I saw a woman on my way here. Down the same path you came from."

"And you're not aware as to where she might've gone?"

"She told me she would be sitting on the side of the road. Waiting for Cullen's men to arrive so she could take them out. Guess, you and your men should consider yourselves lucky she didn't."

Jack gulped and turned back to the soldiers. Whispering something to them as the Outlaw could only watch. Jack nodded and looked back to face the Outlaw and smiled.

"Very well. We'll be on our way to inform Lieutenant Cullen of the news. Take care of yourself, Outlaw."

"I will."

From there, Jack and the solders turned back and rode out of Maverick Town with the Outlaw riding in the opposite direction. Riding back toward the saloon, the Vigilantress stepped out with her eyes facing the entrance the town. When she looked, she saw Jack and the soldiers leaving. A sigh of relief exhaled from her body as the Outlaw looked down at her with a nod of respect.

"They asked for you."

"And you didn't give me up."

"I didn't. No reason why I should've."

"So, what's next?" She questioned. "We both know they'll be back eventually."

"Then, best you prepare yourself for such a time. Meanwhile, I have matters to attend to near the mines. Take care of yourself, my lady."

"I will."

THE LONE KID

The Outlaw rode past Maverick Town and had reached the location of the mines. Taking the moment to stop, he leaped from his horse as he heard the muffling voices of men coming out of the mine. Finding a place to hide himself near the rocks, he watched as two men exited the mine, both carried with them chests. The chests were in similar fashion to those the Outlaw saw when he encountered Weldon's men in the woods.

"His men." The Outlaw whispered.

Before the Outlaw could make a strike, a young man bolted from the other side of the mines, holding a revolver in his hand, aimed at the two men. The men paused in their step seeing the young man.

"What are you going to do with that?" One of the men questioned.

"You're thieves." The young man answered. "You're stealing from the people of Maverick Town. I cannot allow you to leave."

The two men looked at one another and back toward the young man. Within a second's passing the men busted out with laughter. Laughing and patting themselves on the back, confusing the young man. With the revolver in his hand slowly trembling, the two men pulled out revolvers of their own, terrifying the young man as he held his up even higher. The Outlaw couldn't watch any longer and came out from behind the rocks, taking fire at the two men, quickly killing them in mere seconds to the young man's own fear.

"Next time when you try to confront a pair of thieves, do so with much quietness."

The young man gave the Outlaw a nod of understanding. The Outlaw nodded back and asked of the young man's name. the young man sheathed his revolver and stood firm.

"My name is a mystery to the people. I prefer to be called the Lone Kid."

"The Lone Kid?" The Outlaw said with a chuckle. "That so?"

"Is there something wrong with it? Is it childish or not a name thieves would fear?"

"No. it's your name. do so with it as you wish. Just concentrate on honing your skills first. Then the name will take care of itself."

"I'm sorry, sir. But, how do you know all of this?"

"Because. My name, my real name is Clint Winston. However, the people of this land and beyond only know me as the Lone Outlaw."

The young man's jaw dropped like he won some kind of prize out of the blue. The Outlaw knew why he was giving such an expression. He's heard of his actions prior to their meeting and with that information given to him by just a sheer expression, the Outlaw grinned while hanging his head.

"You're him?! The Outlaw who killed the Four Hats!"

"Yes I am."

"But, do you know the good you've done for the people of the city? With the Hats dead, you've provided a better life for the people. They can dwell in their homes without fear. Because of your good deeds, you've given them a glimpse into a life of peace."

"Good to know." The Outlaw replied, turning back toward

his horse.

"Where are you off to now, if I may ask such a thing?" The Kid spoke.

"I came here to stop the thieves. Seems with your interference, that task is done."

"And where are you off to now?"

"Silver City. There's other business that needs tending."

"Well, if I may ask, will you require assistance in your tasks of bringing forth justice?"

The Outlaw looked at the Kid with a hint of humor, yet, he was impressed by the young man's tenacity to join in the fight and to help others. The Outlaw went ahead and told him that he should continue practicing his skills, such as his stealth if he wants to avoid being seen by thieves, bounty hunters, and suchlike. The Outlaw nodded and stepped upon his horse and rode off from the mines.

Back over in Silver City, Thaine remained as Lieutenant Cullen was outside of the city on his military duties with a meeting with the Governor. Thaine went and acquired a brothel of the city with the income arriving from the brothel in Maverick Town. Inside the brothel, Thaine sat in his office as the sounds of a filled bar with prostitutes laughing and men cheering, Thaine began overlooking the papers he took from Cullen's office. Seeing all the details and with mire time to examine them, Thaine had enough. Balling up the papers and tossing them into the fireplace. Thaine sat back in the chair with his head hanging over. His eyes focused on the ceiling as his mind wandered off. Three minutes had passed before Thaine picked up his head, cracking his knuckles and neck. He took another minute to pause and stare into space before his eyes glazed over toward the fireplace, seeing the embers rising from the burning papers.

"Yeah." Thaine said to himself. "I'm going to do it."

THE HIGH COST OF LIVING

Thaine quickly arrived in Silver City and began attacking the officials. From the soldiers of Cullen's command to those who were on other business affairs. Thaine did not care for the civilians as several of them were caught in the crossfire. Moving through Silver City, Thaine made it his mission to cause disruption to all of the towns in the land. With his escape from fire in Silver City, Lieutenant Cullen learned of Thaine's actions and immediately sent out his forces to track him down and kill him on site. Thaine rode off into Maverick Town and had done the same, coming into conflict with a few bounty hunters who were looking for Thaine regarding his past actions of avoiding justice.

"More boys seeking trouble." Thaine cackled.

"You're not getting past us this time around."

"Oh, I think I will."

Thaine took out his revolver and fired a shot, hitting a sack of dynamite near one of the saloon posts which he had placed there before the hunters' confrontation. With the explosion, Thaine took his escape from Maverick Town. Riding off into the unknown, Thaine laughed in the cold air, taking in the thought of Cullen and his soldiers on his trail. A thrill he surely sought.

Elsewhere upon the night, the Outlaw rode into Dodge Town, a place which is familiar to Silver City's aesthetics, although a place where most of the criminals seek to dwell. A town not fit for those who desire a life of peace and happiness in the smallest of matters. As the Outlaw rode into the town, the criminals who sat outside smoking and drinking saw his arrival and quickly ran inside. The Outlaw did not chuckle nor nod toward their responses, he continued moving. Riding toward the front of a hardware store, the Outlaw stepped from his horse and approached the entrance. Upon entering, a sharp kick bolted from the entrance. Knocking the Outlaw back and down the steps into the mud. Rising up without fail, the Outlaw looked up toward the entrance, seeing a man standing with a smirk.

"And you are?" The Outlaw questioned, standing on his feet.

"I've been looking for you. Lieutenant Cullen has promised me something of value if I found you."

CLOSE ENCOUNTERS

Who the Outlaw was staring at was Longshot. Through some trial and errors, he had finally found the famed Lone Outlaw. Grinning as he stared him down, the Outlaw lowered his hand, reaching for his revolver and Longshot began doing the same. Their eyes locked onto one another as they reached for their weapons.

"You think you can draw quicker than me?" Longshot grinned.

"You'll find out soon." The Outlaw replied with a grim face.

Both their hands on the hilts. Their eyes locked. One with a coldness of focus and the other grinning with patience. Before they could raise up their weapons, a woman exited the store, stopping Longshot out of his focus.

"No need to kill him. I heard we might need him. He's valuable."

"And who told you he was valuable alive? Better that he's dead. That way he won't gain an upper-hand on us."

The woman's ruby dress had glistened with the moonlight as she ceased Longshot and faced toward the Outlaw. Unimpressed, he removed his hand from his side and stepped forward to face the woman as Longshot crossed his arms, leaning against the store wall with his eyes solely focused on the Outlaw's hands.

"And who are you?" The Outlaw questioned.

"My name is Ada. Ada Red. I was warned about you."

"And who warned you of me?"

"A good friend I call Weldon. You see, after you paid your visit to him at his place, he sent word to me."

"He sent you to kill me? Why? Couldn't have done it himself?"

"Don't take my lean presence for weakness. He called me because I am one of the most skilled assassins in all the Northern West."

"I've never heard of you. I would have if you claimed yourself to be."

"Because we haven't met and had no reason to meet. Until this night."

"And what will you do now that we've met? Will you seek to kill me like your colleague over there or are you willing to bring me back to Weldon alive? If you even can."

Ada chuckled as she waved her dress, showing the Outlaw her own revolver strapped to her leg. He nodded with impression, yet he's seen such before in his travels. Longshot sighed, pressing against the wall and stepping forward.

"Let's just kill this bastard and be done with it. I want to get paid."

"You will be paid." Ada replied with a smile. "Just have some extra patience."

The sound of a galloping horse began to sound in the distance, gaining the Outlaw's attention. Longshot steadied himself near the steps with his hand on his revolver and Ada done the same. Both ducked down as the Outlaw went to face the coming rider. Seeing nothing but a silhouette through the low-lit darkness, the horse appeared before him and riding into Dodge Town was Thaine. The Outlaw sighed as Thaine saw him. Only responding with a laugh.

"Well, I'll be dammed." Thaine laughed. "The hell are you doing here, Winston?"

"On business. And you're here because?"

"I have my reasons. Besides being hunted down by Cullen's soldiers. Whom I might add are on their way here."

"For what purpose would they come into Dodge Town?"

"I've started some shenanigans and there's no way out of it without a shootout."

"And you've brought the shootout to this place? Yet, not in the wilderness nor the open desert?"

"You know me? Where's there's buildings, there's diversion."

"Every time with you, Tucker. Every damn time."

Thaine looked toward the store, seeing Longshot and Ada standing there with a stare. He nodded before catching a better look at Ada's features. He grinned.

"You didn't tell me you were speaking with such a beautiful woman."

"I'm not here for that."

"Damn shame."

Thane approached the steps before Longshot took out his revolver, aimed toward Thaine's forehead. Thaine's hands raised up with a grin on his face. Ada could only watch as she showed no emotion. Although, she was intrigued by Thaine's characteristics. She saw no fear in him and he saw no fear in her.

"Milady, I would love to know your name."

"Ada Red."

"I see. The dress. It does give off your name. I guess Ada Ruby wasn't working out."

"Red has a better strength to it."

"Alright." Longshot butted in. "Enough, you're Thaine Tucker?"

"I am. Who might you be, boy?"

"Folks call me Longshot. And I'm not your boy."

"Never said you were."

Voices echoed from the nearby woods. Dozens of them. Thaine turned toward the Outlaw and winked. He knew they were Cullen's soldiers and they had arrived into Dodge Town. The Outlaw began to move through the town, warning anyone who remained to either prepare for battle or flee. Most chose to flee out of the fear of facing Cullen's soldiers as their reputation had spread across the Northern West after the news had spread regarding their input into the American Civil War. Winston approached Thaine as the voices inched closer with their footsteps beginning to sound.

"This is your doing. You're not going anywhere."

"Never said I was. This is what I wanted all along. Someone has to show Cullen's who's boss around this land."

He glared up toward Longshot and Ada. Asking if they would join in the fight. Longshot declined and warned him if he would survive the coming shootout they'll meet again. The Outlaw agreed to it as Longshot fled. Ada looked out, seeing the lamps in the trees. She gave Winston and Thaine a wink before taking her leave. Now, only the Outlaw and Thaine remained for the fight as the soldiers began stepping out from the woods and into the town road.

"You're ready for this?" Thaine asked with a grin on his face.

"I am." The Outlaw said coldly.

WAR OF THE WEST

Without fail, the Outlaw rose up his revolvers alongside Thaine as the soldiers stepped forward out of the woods. Walking in front of them was Jack to Thaine's displeasure. He wanted Cullen to have led them. The fact of him not being present drew a sore pain into Thaine's ego. Cullen had other matters to attend to which were bigger than his recent attacks throughout the towns.

"Listen," Jack said. "There's no reason for this to be a shootout. Just hear me out."

"Where is Cullen?!" Thaine screamed. "Where the fuck is he?!"

"He has other business ventures. Your recent actions in certain towns has proven to be of little value for his attention. He sent us to come here for those reasons."

"I'm not listening to some young whippersnapper to tell me what to do!"

"Don't be rash." Winston said. "Let's hear him out before we start shooting."

Thaine sighed.

"Shit. Might as well."

Jack commanded the soldiers behind him to lower their weapons. While they lowered them, Thaine reached for his own revolvers, only to be stopped by Winston. With a shrug, Thaine removed his hands and crossed his arms. Staring a hole through

Jack while gazing the soldiers around him.

"Here's the deal." Jack said, stepping forward. "Lieutenant Cullen has a warrant out for the both of you. But, he's given an offer for you both. Something which will have you to avoid some prison time."

"And what's the pay?" Thaine questioned.

"I'm sorry."

"The pay? What is Cullen going to pay us? He didn't think we'll turn ourselves over for something cheap."

"He's not going to pay you anything. Only give you a free pass."

"Bullshit. I'm only accepting gold. Hell, give me some silver if you have it and I know a man of Cullen's status has some silver laying around."

"He's not going to pay you, Tucker. Never even spoken a word concerning it. Lieutenant Cullen only wants to give you a free pass and that's it."

Thaine chuckled and turned his back toward Jack and the soldiers. The Outlaw kept his eye on Thaine as he was shaking his head and his fingers began to twitch. Thaine began to chuckle and Winston knew what was about to happen. Turning over to look at him, Thaine grinned.

"Get ready."

"Thaine, no."

Tossing back his duster, Thaine turned toward Jack and the soldiers with his revolvers in hand. Jack caught the glisten of the guns in his gaze and quickly dove out of the way as the guns began firing at the soldiers. The soldiers quickly spread themselves around the area as Winston took out his revolvers and fired alongside Thaine as they stepped back before the soldiers could regroup and return fire.

"All you had to do what wait it out!" The Outlaw yelled.

"You know me too well, Winston. I never give in to these fools."

Backing away as they fired, two of the soldiers arose and returned fire with their rifles. Ducking around the stacked logs, Thaine fired back, hitting two soldiers in the chests as Winston fired, taking down several soldiers. As more soldiers fell, others came out of the woods like they were respawning. Jack sat back against the store as he watched the shootout. Taking a way to escape from the firefight, the Outlaw ran toward him and held him against the store wall.

"Don't kill me." Jack said shivering.

"I'm not going to kill you. Only that you send Cullen a message."

"Ok. What is it?"

"Tell him to leave me alone. Otherwise, I'll be coming for his head. I can't speak for Thaine, of course. He's already on that path. Best you warn your lieutenant before Thaine finds him."

The Outlaw tossed Jack to the ground. Backing away, Jack stood up and ran away back into the woods. Sighing as Jack vanished into the trees, Thaine approached him from behind, warning him of the soldiers entering the town as the shooting continued. Thaine pointed toward the woods.

"We have no choice."

"You're right." Winston replied. "Let's hide before they find us."

While seeking to make their way toward another section of the woods, the soldiers entered fully into Dodge Town. Some carried dynamite in their hands and laid it around the buildings. The soldiers didn't care for the town, they already were aware of it being a town for thieves and bandits. To their concern, the destruction of the town would be better as the criminals could no longer hide. Thaine looked back and saw the dynamite, his eyes widen.

"Shit."

"What now?"

"They've got dynamite. We need to go now!"

The dynamite was lit up with the flames as the two gunslingers ran toward the trees, the town exploded behind them. The blast even had enough pressure to toss them both through the trees and into the woods. Laying on the ground and groaning, up in the air was debris of wood falling down like heavy rain. Smoke consumed the air in the distance as they stood up into the silence of the air.

"Dodge Town is gone." Thaine said, looking back through the trees.

"Good riddance." Winston replied. "Thieves deserve no place of refuge."

"What now?"

"We find our way back to Silver City."

"Silver City?" Thaine jumped. "The hell for? Why now Maverick Town?"

"You have something there of value?"

"I have value in every place I go."

The Outlaw grunted with a nod.

Walking into the woods to avoid the soldiers' search party. They found themselves nearing the open road. Thaine sighed as he jumped out onto the road, finding themselves surrounded by the woods behind them and the open desert on the opposite. Hearing hooves nearby, Thaine turned to see Winston standing beside his horse.

"How the hell did you get the horse over here?"

"I sent him off as soon as I met Longshot."

"Damn."

Hearing more sound coming from the woods behind them, Thaine raised up his revolvers as Winston did the same. Waiting to see who was coming out, they paused with their fingers on the triggers. Waiting patiently to see who's approaching them. As they inched closer, Winston sighed, lowering his guns.

"You know them?" Thaine asked.

"I do."

The Outlaw watched as the Vigilantress and the Lone Kid came out of the woods. They greeted each other to Thaine's confusion.

"Why are you both out here?"

"We heard the explosion and wanted to see what happened?" The Kid said.

"I heard word you were heading out to Dodge Town." The Vigilantress replied. "Figured I would come by in case you needed an extra hand."

"We need to get going." Thaine said. "Did either of you bring any extra horses?"

"They did." The Kid said, pointing behind them.

Turning back around to the open desert, they found themselves confronted by a tribe of Natives. All on horseback. Three horses were left to the side for Thaine, the Kid, and the Vigilantress. The Outlaw stared at their leader and he recognized him. The leader nodded toward him and he nodded back.

"*Thunderstroke.*" The Outlaw uttered.

"Lone Outlaw." Thunderstroke spoke, approaching him. "We have matters to discuss."

THE LONE OUTLAW AND HIS ADVENTURES
THROUGHOUT THE NORTHERN WEST SHALL
CONTINUE IN:

ABOUT THE AUTHOR

Ty'Ron W. C. Robinson II is the author of several works of fiction. Including the *Dark Titan Universe Saga*, *The Haunted City Saga*, *EverWar Universe*, *Symbolum Venatores*, *Frightened!*, *Instincts*, *Chevah Mythos*, *The Horde*, *Argoron*, *The Supreme Pursuer*, *Vanok*, *Dark Titan's The Dead Days*, and *Agent Trevor*.

Also of other books (*The Book of The Elect, etc.*) and One-Shot short stories.

More information pertaining to the author and stories can be found at darktitanentertainment.com.

Twitter: @TyRonRobinsonII
Vero: @tyronrobinsonii

Twitter: @DarkTitan_
Instagram: @darktitanentertainment
Facebook: @DarkTitanEnt